ONE BLUE PILL AND A NIGHT FULL OF ECSTASY.
IMPOSSIBLE! I SAW YOUR CAR GO UP IN FLAMES WITH MY OWN EYES!
MIRACLES DO HAPPEN. TAKE A CLOSER LOOK.
BEFORE YOU KILL ME I WANT YOU TO KNOW THAT I ALWAYS SAW YOU AS MY SON.
CAN YOU BELIEVE IT? HE ALWAYS TREATED ME AS HIS SON.
YOU ARE THE BEST FATHER I HAVE KNOWN. YOU TRIED TO BLOW ME UP IN SMOKE.
AF516669

THE OLD MAN WAS TOO SOFT ON HIS ENEMIES. THE WORLD HAS CHANGED. THEY WOULD HAVE KILLED HIM EVENTUALLY.
PIPPI WAS SOFT ON HIS ENEMIES BUT DON SHOWS NO MERCY TO HIS ENEMIES. OF ALL THE PEOPLE, YOU SHOULD HAVE KNOWN BETTER. DON'S ENEMIES ARE BORN WITH EXPIRY DATES. YOU JUST REACHED YOURS.
THE POISON IN THIS SYRINGE IS UNIQUE. YOU WILL KEEP HALLUCINATING TILL YOUR DEATH. IT WILL MAKE YOUR DEATH LESS PAINFUL.
I DON'T ENJOY KILLING PEOPLE. THEY ASK FOR IT. WE CAN GO TO MY PLACE AND YOU CAN HAVE ALL THE FUN YOU PLANNED FOR TONIGHT.
AHHH...

SIX YEARS AGO.
GOLA BAR MUMBAI
JULIE! THE WOMAN OF MY DREAMS. TONIGHT I SHALL PROPOSE TO HER.
MARC! YOU ARE NOT ALLOWED IN HERE. LEAVE NOW!
SHE WILL CRUSH YOUR HEART INTO A THOUSAND PIECES. I SHALL WAIT FOR YOU TO JOIN ME. RAJU BEVDA'S PREDICTIONS ARE ALWAYS TRUE.
I LOVE YOU JULIE. I BROUGHT A GIFT FOR YOU.
YOU GIFT CHEAP IMITATION JEWELLERY TO JULIE, THE HEARTTHROB OF GOLA BAR?
MY ANSWER IS CLEAR. GET LOST FOR YOUR OWN GOOD.
Crush!

HEY BABY! COME TO PAPA!
I HAVE SMUGGLED IT FROM ITALY. NOW IT SHALL ADORN YOUR NECK BABY!
WHO IS THIS JOKER?
A ROADSIDE ROMEO WHO PROCLAIMS HIS LOVE FOR ME. HE IS NOBODY WORTH MENTIONING.
YOU'VE GOT GUTS. YOU COME INSIDE MY DEN AND PROPOSE TO MY GIRL. STAY AWAY FROM MY GIRL OR ELSE YOU WILL BE BURIED ALIVE IN YOUR GRAVE.
A DEATH THREAT! HOW IRONIC. I AM JUST COMING BACK FROM A FUNERAL. LOOK I AM STILL DRESSED IN BLACK.

BLACK IS MY FAVOURITE COLOUR. IT REMINDS ME OF YOUR FUTURE. I WILL HAVE TO WEAR BLACK TO YET ANOTHER FUNERAL.
I SEE THAT MODESTY IS NOT YOUR FORTE. YOU SHALL REGRET THIS DAY FOR THE REST OF YOUR LIFE.
AAH
Thump
I HATE THAT GRIN ON YOUR FACE AND TODAY I SHALL REMOVE IT PERMANENTLY.
Thwap
TAKE HIM AWAY AND SQUASH HIM TO PULP. I DON'T WANT TO RUIN MY IMPORTED SUIT WITH HIS BLOOD. A MAN SHOULD ALWAYS LOOK GOOD ON A DATE.

IN THE BACK ALLEY OF GOLA BAR FOR AN HOUR.
THAT SHOULD BE ENOUGH FOR TODAY.THE NEXT TIME WE SEE YOU IN THIS VICINITY YOU ARE A DEAD MAN.
KILL ME NOW OR FLEE TO A PLACE WHERE I CAN'T FIND YOU. YOUR DAYS ARE NUMBERED. TICK! TOCK! TICK! TOCK!
THE BOSS DOES NOT WANT HIM DEAD. SOMEONE IS COMING. LET'S GET OUT OF HERE.
MARC'S SAVIOUR WAS NONE OTHER THAN HIS FRIEND RAJU BEVDA.
YOU WERE RIGHT BEVDA. SHE DOES NOT LOVE ME.
KEEP YOUR MOUTH SHUT FOR A MOMENT. YOU ARE LUCKY TO BE ALIVE AFTER PROPOSING TO THE MOLL OF A RUTHLESS MOBSTER. HE IS TOO POWERFUL.

IT TOOK TWO MONTHS FOR MARC TO RECOVER.
REVENGE TASTES BEST WHEN SERVED COLD. TICK! TOCK!
DID YOU MAKE A WILL MY FRIEND? IF NOT, THEN DON'T BOTHER.
TICK! TOCK!
ONE FATAL WOUND IN ANY OF THE VITAL ORGANS MEANS DEATH. YOUR TIME IS UP. TICK! TOCK!
I MAY FORGET THE FACE OF A MAN BUT I NEVER FORGET THE PLACE I BURY HIM. ONE DOWN, ONE TO GO.
TWO HOURS LATER...
YOU SHOULD HAVE KILLED ME WHILE YOU HAD THE CHANCE. DON'T EXPECT ANY MERCY FROM THE APOSTLE OF DEATH.
CALL IT FATE! HAD YOU NOT CROSSED MY PATH, YOU WOULD HAVE DIED AN OLD MAN.

BILLA IS DEAD AND RANA IS MISSING. SURELY RANA HAS GONE UNDERGROUND AFTER KILLING BILLA. FIND THAT BASTARD AND BRING HIM TO ME. I WILL DEAL WITH HIM PERSONALLY.
CHEERS ON EXECUTING SUCH A CUNNING PLAN TO PERFECTION. SHETTY IS LOOKING FOR RANA. HE BELIEVES THAT RANA MURDERED BILLA AND HAS GONE UNDERGROUND. NOW YOU ARE FREE TO TAKE HIM DOWN.
WE ANTICIPATED THAT, DIDN'T WE? KILLING THE BODYGUARDS WAS EASY. IT WILL BE DIFFICULT TO REACH SHETTY.
THERE IS A BIG CHINK IN SHETTY'S ARMOUR. SHETTY DOES HIS ENTIRE TRANSACTIONS WITH THIS FOREIGNER. HIS NAME IS SILVIO. SILVIO IS ITALIAN. CURRENTLY HE IS IN INDIA. A BIG TRANSACTION IS ABOUT TO TAKE PLACE. THIS MAKES SHETTY VULNERABLE.
DO YOU HAVE ANY CLUE ABOUT THEIR TRANSACTIONS?
SILVIO IS SMUGGLING IN A HUGE CONSIGNMENT OF GOLD. THE CONSIGNMENT WILL REACH THE ABANDONED DOCK AT NIGHT TOMORROW. SHETTY IS MOST VULNERABLE DURING THE TRANSFER OF THE CONSIGNMENT. HE WILL BE THERE PERSONALLY.
AN HOUR LATER...
INSPECTOR KAMBLE. YOU ARE ABOUT TO GET A PROMOTION. ARE YOU INTERESTED?
DIG UP ALL INFORMATION ABOUT SILVIO. FIND OUT WHERE HE IS STAYING. I WILL TAKE CARE OF SHETTY.

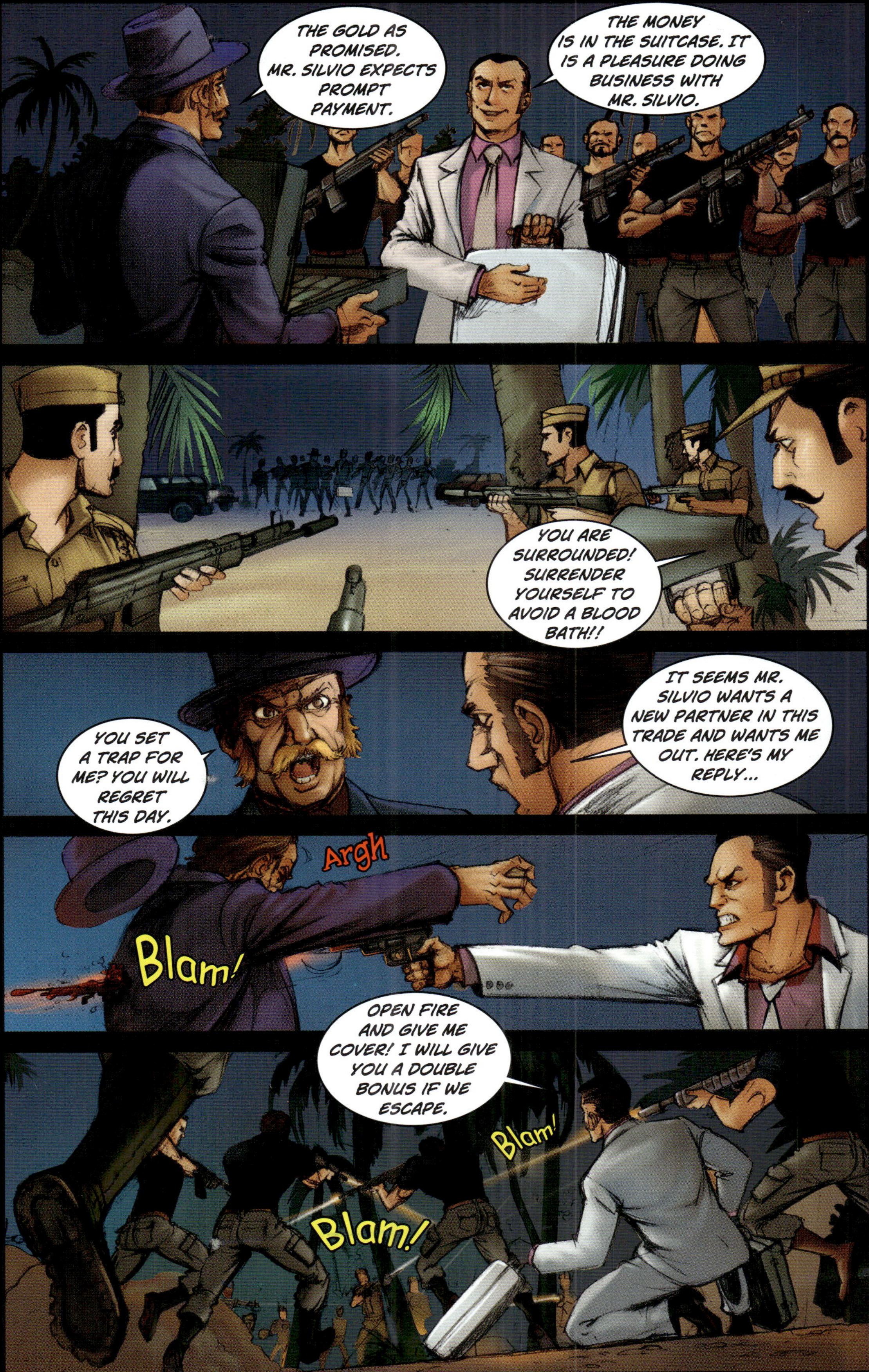
THE GOLD AS PROMISED. MR. SILVIO EXPECTS PROMPT PAYMENT.
THE MONEY IS IN THE SUITCASE. IT IS A PLEASURE DOING BUSINESS WITH MR. SILVIO.
YOU ARE SURROUNDED! SURRENDER YOURSELF TO AVOID A BLOOD BATH!!
YOU SET A TRAP FOR ME? YOU WILL REGRET THIS DAY.
IT SEEMS MR. SILVIO WANTS A NEW PARTNER IN THIS TRADE AND WANTS ME OUT. HERE'S MY REPLY...
Argh
Blam!
OPEN FIRE AND GIVE ME COVER! I WILL GIVE YOU A DOUBLE BONUS IF WE ESCAPE.
Blam!
Blam!

Blam!
Argh
ALMOST THERE!
THAT WAS CLOSE. I EVADED DEATH BY A WHISKER.
YOU HAVE EVADED DEATH BUT HOW WILL YOU EVADE ME. STOP THE CAR AT THE NEXT TURN. YOU HAVE REACHED YOUR DESTINATION.
EASY WITH THE KNIFE. I WILL STOP THE CAR.
TIME TO GET DOWN!
HELP!

SPARE MY LIFE. YOU CAN KEEP MY MONEY AND GOLD. I PROMISE I WILL NEVER SEEK REVENGE AGAINST YOU!
I NEVER TRUST THE PROMISES OF A DESPERATE MAN. I KILL MY ENEMIES WHEN I HAVE THEM AT MY MERCY. IT ELIMINATES CHANCES OF RETALIATION.
YOU WILL FIND THIS GRAVE COMFORTABLE. I DUG IT PERSONALLY FOR YOU.
I WILL GIVE YOU A FIGHTING CHANCE TO LIVE. IF YOU COME OUT OF THIS GRAVE, I WILL LET YOU LIVE.
I CAN'T ...... BREA...... HEL.... UFF....!
SHETTY NEVER MADE IT OUT OF THE GRAVE.

AN HOUR LATER...
COME OUT OF THE CAR.
IS THERE A PROBLEM OFFICER?
YOU ARE UNDER ARREST FOR SMUGGLING GOLD. NOW GET OUT OF THE CAR!
HOW CAN I BE GUILTY OF A CRIME IF YOU CAN'T CATCH ME?
Slam
INSPECTOR KAMBLE WAS IN HOT PURSUIT OF MARC.

KRRASH
SURRENDER NOW! YOU CANNOT ESCAPE THE LAW!!
DO YOURSELF A FAVOUR INSPECTOR. STAY OUT OF MY WAY.
CRASHH
THUD
YOU MADE THE WRONG CHOICE INSPECTOR. I CAN'T LOSE. IT'S LIKE A CURSE.

BAD NEWS. THERE WAS A POLICE RAID. OUR AGENT WAS KILLED. SHETTY FLED FROM THE SCENE WITH THE GOLD. MOST OF HIS MEN ARE EITHER DEAD OR BEHIND BARS.
SUCH REVERSALS ARE PART OF OUR BUSINESS. FIND SHETTY. I WANT MY MONEY.
DON'T BOTHER LOOKING FOR A DEAD MAN.
WHO ARE YOU? HOW DID YOU COME IN? DIDN'T THE GUARDS STOP YOU?
THEY CHOSE TO CALL IT A DAY AND CATCH UP WITH THEIR SLEEP. CAN I GET A DRINK? AFTER ALL, I HAVE BROUGHT GIFTS FOR YOUR BOSS. CHECK THE BRIEFCASES.
HOW DARE YOU!
RELAX! SHOW ME THE BRIEFCASE.
OUR GOLD!
THIS YOUNG MAN HAS EARNED HIS DRINK. SERVE HIM THE FINEST WINE AND LEAVE US ALONE.

I UNDERSTAND THE REASON BEHIND RETURNING THE BRIEFCASE FILLED WITH GOLD. WHY DID YOU BRING THE CASE FULL OF CASH?
YOU ARE A MAN OF CONSIDERABLE POWER AND INFLUENCE. I WANT YOU TO INVEST THIS MONEY FOR ME. I WANT TO PLAY IN THE BIG LEAGUE.
YOU ARE DESTINED FOR GREAT THINGS. I RAISE A TOAST TO YOUR SUCCESS.
WHAT ABOUT THE POLICE? THEY ARE IN HOT PURSUIT!
WE SHALL LEAVE THIS COUNTRY BEFORE THE POLICE CAN HUNT US DOWN. TILL THEN YOU ARE MY GUEST.
THIS IS YOUR PASSPORT AND VISA. WE ARE GOING TO ITALY. I SHALL INTRODUCE YOU TO THE MAN WHO CAN MENTOR YOU TO YOUR DESTINY. YOU ARE ABOUT TO START A NEW AND GLAMOROUS LIFE, FAR AWAY FROM THE SLUMS OF MUMBAI.
I, ME AND MYSELF MAKE A GREAT TEAM. THE FUTURE LOOKS PROMISING.

ITALY...
DON PIPPI, MARC NEEDS YOUR GUIDANCE. HE HAS EXCEPTIONAL TALENT AND NEEDS AN OPPORTUNITY TO PLAY IN THE BIG LEAGUE.
WE ARE HAVING PROBLEMS WITH A POLICE OFFICER. HE IS HONEST AND BRAVE. TAKE CARE OF HIM. ALEXANDRO WILL EXPLAIN THE DETAILS OF THIS JOB TO YOU.
MY FRIEND SPEAKS HIGHLY OF YOU. I AM READY TO MENTOR YOU BUT WHAT DO I GET IN RETURN?
I PROMISE MY UNWAVERING LOYALTY TO YOU. YOUR ENEMIES SHALL BE MY ENEMIES AND THEY WILL RUE THE DAY THEY DECIDE TO CROSS PATHS WITH YOU.
CONSIDER IT DONE. BUT I DON'T NEED A BABY SITTER TO WATCH MY BACK. I WILL EXECUTE THE PLAN MY WAY.
YOU SHALL HAVE A FREE HAND.

HELLO OFFICER. CARE FOR A DRINK?
OH MY GOD! TESS!
IT'S A MANNEQUIN. I DON'T UNDERSTAND!
RELAX OFFICER. YOUR WIFE IS SAFE AND WAITING FOR YOU AT HER FAVOURITE RESTAURANT. APPARENTLY YOU HAVE DECIDED TO GIVE HER A TREAT SO I WILL KEEP THIS MEETING BRIEF.
PERSONALLY I LIKE MEN WHO WON'T BE BOUGHT. IT'S CHEAPER TO KILL THEM. HOWEVER DON PIPPI VALUES AN HONEST MAN LIKE YOU. HE OFFERS HIS FRIENDSHIP.
I WILL VISIT THE DON PERSONALLY AND THANK HIM FOR SPARING ME AND MY FAMILY.
MAN ALWAYS HAS A CHOICE. SUBMISSION OR DEATH. YOU MADE A WISE CHOICE. NOW RUSH. YOUR WIFE IS WAITING FOR YOU.

MARC! EXCELLENT WORK! THE OFFICER LEFT A WHILE AGO. WE GAINED A VALUABLE ALLY IN THE LAW ENFORCEMENT DEPARTMENT.
MARC, MEET MY DAUGHTER FLORENCE. SHE IS A LAWYER AND ASSISTS ME IN MY BUSINESS.
HELLO MARC.
HI.
DAD IS RIGHT. YOU ARE THE MAN HE WANTED ALL ALONG. ALL YOU LACK IS FINESSE.
I DON'T UNDERSTAND.
I HAVE BUILT AN EMPIRE BUT I HAVE NO SUCCESSOR. I AM OLD FASHIONED AND HATE UNNECESSARY BLOODSHED. YOU ARE LETHAL AND PERSUASIVE WHICH IS A RARE COMBINATION. I WANT TO GROOM YOU AS MY SUCCESSOR. ALEXANDRO IS LOYAL BUT LACKS LEADERSHIP SKILLS AND HAS A HOT HEAD.
FLORENCE, EXPLAIN OUR BUSINESS TO HIM. HE MUST UNDERSTAND EVERY SMALL INTRICACY.
I WILL DAD. HE WILL MAKE AN EXCELLENT PROTÉGÉ. I MIGHT TAKE HIM ON A TOUR OF THE COUNTRYSIDE IF HE COMES UP TO MY EXPECTATIONS.

THE BETTING SYNDICATE IS REFUSING TO PAY US THE PERCENTAGE ACCORDING TO OUR DEAL. THEY WANT TO RENEGOTIATE. OTHER FAMILIES ARE ENTERING OUR TERRITORY. THEY THINK WE ARE WEAK. LET US SET AN EXAMPLE BY TEACHING A HARSH LESSON TO THE SYNDICATE.
DID I MISS SOMETHING?
VIOLENCE IS TO BE USED AS A LAST RESORT.
THIS IS NONE OF YOUR BUSINESS.
THE GAMBLING SYNDICATE IS GIVING YOU A ROUGH TIME. BUT THE PROBLEM IS TRIVIAL. TRY A LEMONADE. IT WILL COOL YOUR HEAD.
NOT ALL THE MEMBERS OF THE SYNDICATE WISH TO REVOLT. I PROPOSE TO IDENTIFY THE ROTTEN APPLE AND DEAL WITH HIM PERSONALLY. THE REST WILL FALL IN LINE.
WHAT DO YOU PROPOSE?
VERY WELL. DEAL WITH THE GAMBLING SYNDICATE DIRECTLY. YOU HAVE A FREE HAND. ALEXANDRO WILL NOT INTERFERE IN YOUR PLAN.
MARC HAS WHAT IT NEEDS TO BECOME A GREAT DON. YOU CANNOT SUBDUE PEOPLE LIKE MARC. THEY ARE BORN TO RULE. ALEXANDRO WILL HAVE TO ACCEPT HIM AS HIS LEADER SOONER OR LATER.
YOU ARE PUTTING TOO MUCH FAITH IN MARC. ALEXANDRO IS FEELING MARGINALIZED. YOU CAN'T RISK A REVOLT OR DEFECTION.

DON PIPPI IS HURT BY YOUR BEHAVIOR. WE HAVE BEEN PARTNERS FOR YEARS AND I AM SURE WE CAN COME TO A REASONABLE SETTLEMENT.
HERE IS HOW WE WILL SETTLE IT! GO AND TELL YOUR OLD MAN THAT WE WILL PAY ONLY FIVE PERCENT OF OUR TAKINGS. IF YOU PRESS FOR TEN PERCENT WE WILL JOIN HANDS WITH OTHER MAFIA FAMILIES. DON PIPPI IS A SPENT FORCE.
MR. ANTONIO. DOES OLIVER SPEAK FOR THE ENTIRE SYNDICATE?
WE ARE FACING HUGE LOSSES DUE TO POLICE RAIDS. THE PROFITS HAVE SHRUNK. MR. OLIVER HAS EXTREME VIEWS BUT THE ENTIRE SYNDICATE WOULD REQUEST DON PIPPI TO RECONSIDER HIS STANCE.
DON PIPPI WILL TAKE CARE OF THE POLICE OFFICIALS. AS FOR MR. OLIVER'S OBJECTIONS ....
LET'S SAY HE WON'T BE BOTHERING US WITH HIS VIEWS. DON PIPPI HAS PROVED HIS FRIENDSHIP BY ELIMINATING YOUR COMPETITOR MR. ANTONIO. IT'S YOUR TURN TO RECIPROCATE.
I AM GRATEFUL TO DON PIPPI FOR SOLVING MY PROBLEM. OLIVER WAS TRYING TO USURP MY POSITION BY THREATENING AND INSTIGATING OTHER MEMBERS OF THE SYNDICATE. WITH ONE PARTNER LESS TO PAY, I PROPOSE TO PAY 12 PERCENT OF THE REVENUES AS A GIFT OF APPRECIATION TO DON PIPPI.
I DON'T WANT TO SHARE OLIVER'S FATE. I SHALL REMAIN LOYAL TO DON PIPPI AND YOU FOR THE REST OF MY LIFE. CONVEY MY REGARDS TO DON PIPPI.
DON PIPPI WILL BE PLEASED BY YOUR GENEROSITY BUT REMEMBER THAT IF YOU BREAK MY TRUST, I WILL BREAK YOUR NECK. I WILL SURVIVE BUT YOU WON'T.
FLORENCE WHAT ARE YOU DOING HERE?
YOU HAVE BEEN AVOIDING ME FOR THE LAST FEW DAYS. AND I HAVE COME HERE TO FIND OUT THE REASON. I LOVE YOU AND I CAN'T BEAR YOUR INDIFFERENT ATTITUDE.

FLORENCE! DUCK!
BLAM!
ARGH!
THEY WILL GET AWAY! WHAT WERE YOU THINKING ANYWAY? IT WAS FOOLISH OF YOU TO COME HERE.
BLAM!
OK YOU CAN HAVE YOUR ANSWER NOW. I CANNOT RECIPROCATE YOUR FEELINGS. I HOLD YOUR FATHER IN HIGH ESTEEM AND WILL NOT ACT AGAINST HIS WISHES. BESIDES I AM NOT HUSBAND MATERIAL.
YOUR FATHER IS WORRIED. WHERE WERE YOU?
WE WERE ATTACKED BY UNKNOWN ARMED MEN. MARC SAVED MY LIFE.
STAY AWAY FROM HER. SHE IS MY GIRL.
TAKE MY ADVICE. WHEN YOU LIKE A GIRL, PROPOSE BEFORE SOMEBODY ELSE DOES.

THIS IS A MATTER OF GRAVE CONCERN. OUR ENEMIES HAVE BECOME AUDACIOUS. THANK YOU FOR SAVING THE LIFE OF MY DAUGHTER.
SHE IS EQUALLY PRECIOUS TO ME. DON'T WORRY, SHE IS SAFE WITH ME.
I WANT YOU TO GO TO PARIS AND HELP IN EXPANDING OUR CASINO AND BANKING BUSINESS IN EUROPE. TAKE FLORENCE WITH YOU. ONCE THE EXPANSION IS COMPLETE, I WILL JOIN YOU THERE.
I WANT TO HELP. LET ME STAY BACK AND FIGHT THIS WAR WITH YOU.
I HAVE PLANNED GREAT THINGS FOR YOU. YOU CANNOT THROW IT AWAY ON A STUPID GANG WAR.
I WILL NOT LEAVE YOU ALONE, ESPECIALLY AFTER THE ATTACK. BESIDES, YOU NEED ME!
OH! I THOUGHT YOU WOULD LIKE TO STAY CLOSE TO MARC.
FAMILY COMES FIRST. I WILL NOT LEAVE YOU ALONE IN A CRISIS.
YOU WILL NEED A FRESH PASSPORT. I RECOMMEND YOU CHOOSE A NEW NAME TO AVOID SUSPICION.
HOW ABOUT DON? I LIKE THAT NAME.
VERY WELL. I WILL LEAVE YOU TWO ALONE TO BID FAREWELL TO EACH OTHER. THE STEAMER LEAVES IN THE MORNING.
I AM SORRY FLORENCE. DON'T WAIT FOR ME. FIND A SUITABLE GUY AND SETTLE DOWN.
I AM AN OPTIMIST. I WILL KEEP WAITING FOR YOU TILL I DIE.
MARC ASSUMED THE NAME 'DON' AND LEFT FOR PARIS THE NEXT DAY.

PARIS...
LADIES AND GENTLEMEN, I GIVE YOU THE BIGGEST CASINO ON THIS SIDE OF THE ATLANTIC. YOUR FORTUNE AWAITS YOU. WELCOME TO CASINO SICILY.
WITHIN THE SPAN OF A YEAR, DON EXPANDED PIPPI'S CASINO AND BANKING BUSINESSES BY 300%. HE HAD SURPASSED PIPPI'S EXPECTATIONS.

CONGRATULATIONS DON. THREE CASINOS IN THREE MONTHS IS PHENOMENAL SUCCESS. YOU'RE GAINING QUITE A REPUTATION IN OUR CIRCLE. IF THE RUMOURS ARE TRUE THEN YOU ARE POISED FOR GREATER HEIGHTS.
SO YOU ARE A MAN WHO TRUSTS RUMOURS?
OFTEN RUMOURS HAVE AN ELEMENT OF TRUTH IN THEM. I HAVE KEPT YOU ON MY RADAR FOR A LONG TIME. YOU ARE A MAN OF ACTION. WE CAN HAVE A SUCCESSFUL COLLABORATION. IN FACT, I HAVE AN OFFER YOU CANNOT REFUSE.
I AM LISTENING.
I AM SORRY TO INTERFERE BUT WE HAVE A CRISIS. MONSIEUR ALEXANDRO JUST CALLED FROM SICILY. THERE WAS AN ASSASSINATION ATTEMPT ON DON PIPPI. HE IS FATALLY WOUNDED WHILE MADEMOISELLE FLORENCE HAS SUCCUMBED TO BULLET INJURIES.
BOOK MY NEXT FLIGHT TO ROME. I MUST ....
MONSIEUR ALEXANDRO HAS CAUTIONED YOU NOT TO GO TO SICILY. YOUR ENEMIES ARE KEEPING AN EYE ON AIRPORTS AND SEAPORTS.
GET ME A CHARTERED PLANE. I WILL DROP STRAIGHT INTO HIS MANSION.

WE ARE HAVING PROBLEMS WITH A POLICE OFFICER. HE IS HONEST AND BRAVE. TAKE CARE OF HIM. ALEXANDRO WILL EXPLAIN THE DETAILS OF THIS JOB TO YOU.
AFTER I DECIMATE MY ENEMIES, I SHALL COME BACK TO REPAY THIS DEBT.
WE HAVE REACHED THE LOCATION. JUMP!
HOLD YOUR FIRE! I AM AN ALLY.
YOU ARE THE CRAZIEST PERSON I HAVE EVER KNOWN. YOU ALMOST GOT YOURSELF KILLED! COME IN. DON PIPPI WILL NOT LIVE FOR LONG.
I NEED TO SEE FLORENCE FIRST.

DON PIPPI WAS EXTREMELY POPULAR. THERE WAS A HUGE TURNOUT AT THE FUNERAL.
I AM SORRY FOR YOUR LOSS DON. I KNOW THAT THIS IS NOT A GOOD TIME BUT THE HEADS OF THREE MAFIA FAMILIES OF SICILY WANT TO DISCUSS A TRUCE OFFER WITH YOU. THEY WANT TO AVOID FURTHER BLOODSHED. IN MY OPINION YOU SHOULD LISTEN TO THEIR PROPOSAL. I WILL GUARANTEE YOUR PERSONAL SAFETY.
VERY WELL. SET UP A MEETING.
YOU CANNOT FIGHT OUR COMBINED STRENGTH. DON'T TRY SOMETHING FOOLISH, WHICH YOU WILL REGRET FOR THE REST OF YOUR LIFE.
I WILL WAIT FOR YOUR CALL.
FAREWELL MY LOVE.
FLORENCE
IT'S TIME TO LEAVE. ALL ARRANGEMENTS HAVE BEEN MADE.

WE WILL STRIKE AND WIPE THEM OFF BEFORE THEY CAN DEVISE A STRATEGY TO CHOKE US INTO SUBMISSION. THEY THINK THAT DON PIPPI WAS A FOOL. HE HAD MADE PLANS FOR SUCH CONTINGENCIES. WE SHALL AVENGE HIS DEATH. YOU OWE IT TO YOUR DON.
OUR ENEMIES ARE REGROUPING IN A PRIVATE RESORT. IT HAS BEEN TURNED INTO A FORTRESS. TEAM ONE WILL ENTER THE COMPLEX IN A CATERING VAN AND CREATE A DIVERSION BY PLANTING EXPLOSIVES AROUND THE COMPLEX. I WILL LEAD TEAM TWO WHICH WILL ATTACK THE MAIN GATES AND KEEP THEM ENGAGED. THIS WILL ALLOW DON TO LEAD HIS TEAM AND ATTACK FROM THE AIR.
NOT A SINGLE MAN SHOULD ESCAPE OUR BULLETS.
PERFECT. EVERYTHING IS WORKING ACCORDING TO PLAN. WE WILL LAUNCH A SURPRISE ATTACK ON OUR ENEMIES WHEN THEY ARE IN TOTAL DISARRAY.
BLAM! BLAM!
RATA RATARAT

RATA
RA
ZING
ARGH

THE FUTURE IS UNPREDICTABLE UNLESS YOU ARE ME. BUT YOU KNEW THAT ALREADY. TIME TO DIE!!
RATA RATARAT
BLAM!
BLAM!
DON AND HIS TEAM BUTCHERED EVERY ADVERSARY IN THAT ROOM.

WE WIPED OUT THREE MAFIA CLANS. DON PIPPI'S DEATH HAS BEEN AVENGED.
NOT YET MY FRIEND. THERE REMAINS ONE TRAITOR WHO MUST BE PUNISHED FOR BETRAYING OUR TRUST. HE WILL CONTACT YOU SOON. SET THE TRAP FOR HIM.
WHY DID YOU CALL ME HERE? WHAT DO YOU WANT FROM ME?
I NEED PROTECTION FROM DON. I AM WILLING TO PAY ANY PRICE IF YOU ENSURE MY SAFETY. LOOK, I AM SORRY ABOUT FLORENCE. I KNOW YOU HAD A SWEET SPOT FOR HER. TRUST ME, SHE WAS COLLATERAL DAMAGE. BUT NOW YOU HAVE A CHANCE TO FULFILL YOUR DREAM.
DON IS THE ROOT CAUSE OF THIS TRAGEDY. DON PIPPI WAS ABOUT TO BROKER PEACE WITH THE THREE MAFIA FAMILIES BEFORE HE MET DON. HE CHANGED HIS MIND AFTER MEETING DON AND GROOMED HIM TO BE HIS SUCCESSOR, IGNORING YOU. THIS TRAGEDY COULD HAVE BEEN AVERTED HAD PIPPI MADE PEACE WITH THE MAFIA FAMILIES.
IF YOU KILL DON, YOU WILL BE THE NEW HEAD OF THE FAMILY. I CAN HELP YOU TO CONSOLIDATE YOUR RULE AND OPEN NEW AVENUES OF BUSINESS ABROAD.
I AGREE. WE HAVE TO KILL DON.
MY MEN WILL GUARD THIS PLACE AND OFFER YOU PROTECTION. DON'T MOVE OUT OF THIS HOUSE TILL I SAY SO. I WILL INFORM YOU ONCE I MAKE A FOOLPROOF PLAN TO ASSASSINATE DON.

THREE DAYS LATER...
ALEXANDRO, YOU ARE A MAN OF YOUR WORDS. YOU SHALL MAKE A GREAT MAFIA LEADER. WHAT DO YOU WANT IN RETURN FOR SAVING MY LIFE AND KILLING MY NEMESIS?
THE REWARD SHOULD BE IN ACCORDANCE TO THE COMPLEXITY OF THE TASK.
YES INDEED! AND I WILL REWARD YOU WITH SOMETHING BEYOND YOUR DREAMS. FOLLOW ME.
THIS IS MY PRIVATE TREASURE AND YOUR SHARE IS TWENTY PERCENT. YOU CAN PICK ANYTHING YOU LIKE. IN THAT VAULT I HAVE THE NAMES OF CONTACTS AND FILES OF MY TRANSACTIONS. YOU CAN BE MY SUCCESSOR ONE DAY AND HAVE ACCESS TO THEM.
THIS CALLS FOR A BIG CELEBRATION!
A GREAT EVENING LIKE THIS CALLS FOR A GREAT END.
IT DEFINITELY DOES.
GOODNIGHT MY FRIEND.
I WILL COME TO YOUR PLACE IN THE MORNING. YOU WON'T NEED MY PROTECTION ANY MORE.

HE IS ALL YOURS DON. I HAVE DONE EVERYTHING AS YOU COMMANDED.
I WON'T TAKE LONG.
I LOVE THE LOOK OF FEAR, FOR IT SHOWS YOU YOUR TRUE POWER. SILVIO, YOU SHOULD HAVE DONE YOURSELF A FAVOUR. YOU SHOULD HAVE STAYED OUT OF MY PATH. YOUR DEATH WILL BECOME A PART OF DON'S FOLKLORE.
TEN MINUTES LATER ...
LOYALTY IS A RARE TRAIT AND NEEDS TO BE REWARDED. YOU CAN KEEP THE REWARD SILVIO PROMISED YOU AND SEND ME THE REST. I ALSO MAKE YOU THE HEAD OF OUR FAMILY. I WILL BE TAKING OVER DON PIPPI'S GAMBLING OPERATIONS AND BANKS IN EUROPE. YOU CAN CONTROL THE ENTIRE OPERATIONS IN SICILY AND ITALY.
YOU SHALL ALWAYS REMAIN MY LEADER DON. I SWEAR MY ALLEGIANCE TO YOU.

A WEEK LATER ....
WELCOME TO MY HUMBLE RESORT. LET'S TALK IN MY COTTAGE.
I LIKE THIS HUMBLE RESORT. HOW MUCH WILL IT COST ME TO GET ONE OF THESE COTTAGES?
YOU GET IT FOR FREE. I HAVE AN IRRESISTIBLE DEAL FOR YOU.
MACAU ....
I WORK FOR A HUGE SYNDICATE RUN BY A MAN NAMED BORIS. WE EARNED A FORTUNE SELLING ARMS FROM THE BALTIC COUNTRIES AFTER THE DISINTEGRATION OF THE SOVIET UNION. NOW WE HAVE DIVERSIFIED INTO DRUGS, WHICH IS A HIGHLY PROFITABLE BUSINESS. BUT NOW I HAVE A PROBLEM. BORIS IS ABOUT TO RETIRE FROM THE BUSINESS AND PLANS TO HAND OVER THE CONTROL OF THIS SYNDICATE TO MY ARCH RIVAL VARDHAAN.
YOU WANT ME TO ELIMINATE BORIS AND USURP THE CONTROL OF THE SYNDICATE? INTERESTING! NOW LET'S HEAR YOUR OFFER.
YES. YOU HAVE THAT X FACTOR TO SUCCEED PLUS YOU ARE AN UNKNOWN VARIABLE IN THE EQUATION. AFTER YOU FINISH BORIS, I WILL TAKE OVER THE SYNDICATE. VARDHAAN WILL VANISH INTO OBLIVION WITHOUT BORIS'S BACKING. I WILL GIVE YOU CARTE BLANCHE TO RUN THE SHOW.

YOU ARE ONE HELL OF A BUSINESSMAN. YOU KEEP YOUR END OF THE BARGAIN AND I WILL ENSURE THAT BORIS NEVER BOTHERS YOU AGAIN.
NARANG COME INTO MY ROOM. BRING ANITA ALONG.
MR. SINGHANIA WHO IS HE?
HIS NAME IS DON. HE SHALL BE THE NEW OPERATING CHIEF OF THE SYNDICATE ONCE WE ELIMINATE BORIS.
I CAN LEND YOU MY BEST MEN FOR THE ASSASSINATION ATTEMPT. BORIS IS PARANOID ABOUT HIS SECURITY. INSTEAD OF A HOTEL, HE LIVES ON A FORTIFIED YACHT.
EVERY SECURITY RING CAN BE PENETRATED. JUST HIT ON THE WEAK SPOT.
HOW MANY MEN DO YOU NEED FOR THIS MISSION?
I, ME AND MYSELF MAKE A GREAT TEAM. I DON'T NEED OTHER MEMBERS ON MY TEAM. TELL ME THE LOCATION OF THE YACHT AND WAIT FOR MY CALL.

NEXT DAY...
SMOKING CIGARETTES CAN KILL YOU.
PUTT
PUTT
ARGH!
TICK! TOCK! TICK! TOCK!

WARN MR. BORIS! WE ARE UNDER ATTACK.
PHUT PHUT
AAH
HOW GULLIBLE CAN PEOPLE BE...
EIYAAH!
BRAT A RATAT
PHUT PHUT
FOR A MAN WHO DEALT IN GUNS, YOU HAVE PATHETIC AIM. OOPS! IT'S TIME TO LEAVE. I PROMISED ANITA SOME FIREWORKS.

KABOOM
DID YOU LIKE THE FIREWORKS BABY?
IT WAS JUST LIKE YOU PROMISED.
YOU DESERVE TO BE OUR LEADER. I NEVER BELIEVED THAT YOU COULD PULL THIS OFF SOLO.
I CAN'T LOSE. IT'S LIKE A CURSE.
POWER IS A DRUG AND I HOLD ITS PATENT. NOW I AM READY TO TAKE THE WORLD BY STORM.
SURE! YOU SHALL BECOME THE EMPEROR OF OUR TRADE. IN FACT I HAVE AN ASSIGNMENT FOR YOU. ONE OF OUR DEALERS IS TRYING TO SQUEEZE US OUT OF BUSINESS IN PARIS.

ONE ROTTEN APPLE CAN SPOIL THE ENTIRE BASKET. I DON'T WANT ANY ROTTEN APPLES IN MY BASKET. I WILL PERSUADE DJ PERSONALLY.
TWO DAYS LATER ...
PARIS IS FULL OF SCENIC BEAUTY. NO WONDER IT IS CALLED THE CITY OF LOVE.
IT'S TIME.
BUZZ
MOTOROLA
DON!
TO BE CONTINUED...